NO.1 BOY DETECTIVE

The Popstar's Wedding

Collect all the No. 1 Boy Detective books!

NO.1 BOY DETECTIVE

The Popstar's Wedding

Barbara Mitchelhill
Illustrated by
Tony Ross

Andersen Press • London

For Tom who likes football
and Alexandra who loves pink

This edition first published in 2017 by
Andersen Press Limited
20 Vauxhall Bridge Road
London SW1V 2SA
www.andersenpress.co.uk

First published by Andersen Press Limited in 2002

2 4 6 8 10 9 7 5 3

British Library Cataloguing in Publication Data available.

ISBN 978 1 78344 663 6

Printed and bound in Turkey by Omur Printing Co, Istanbul

Chapter 1

My name is Drooth. Damian Drooth.
Crime-buster extraordinaire. Ace
detective.

Let me tell you about my latest case.

It started when a letter arrived
for Mum. It was addressed to Mrs
Drooth, Home Cooking Unlimited.

'Guess who this is from!' she
shrieked. I could tell she was in a real
tizz.

So I read the letter.

Dear Mrs Drooth,
I was wondering if you would be interested in providing the food for my wedding. Perhaps you could come to see me and discuss the menu.
Yours sincerely,
Tiger Lilly

I stared at the signature. I was gobsmacked.

'**Tiger Lilly?**' I yelled. (It was difficult to stay calm.) '**The singer? One of the Bay Babes?**'

Mum nodded and my head exploded. She was my most favourite singer EVER! I was her NUMERO UNO fan! Wow! Wow! Wow!

That morning, Mum telephoned Tiger Lilly and arranged a meeting.

'I'll come with you,' I said.

'I don't think so,' said Mum as she wrote the date in her diary.

'You might get lost,' I insisted.

'I can read a map, Damian.'

'I could be your secretary and take notes.'

'I don't want a secretary.'

I tried a different approach.

'Right! I'll go on hunger strike if you don't take me!'

Mum sighed. 'Don't be stupid, Damian!' she said. 'NO!'

In the end, she gave in. My mum's brain power is no match for my razor-sharp cunning.

And so I got to meet the fabulous Tiger Lilly.

Chapter 2

Tiger Lilly's place was mega huge!
Even the drive was longer than our
street. As we pulled up outside the
front door, there she was waiting for us
on the steps. A Star! Some guys would
have gone wild. But not me! Fame
doesn't bother me. Even though her
eyes were deep blue and her hair was
blonde and right down to her waist – I
stayed cool.

Then Mum spoke.

'This is my little boy, Damian,' she said in her mumsy voice. 'I hope you don't mind him coming with me. There was no one to look after him – and he's inclined to get into trouble.'

I ask you! Embarrassing or what? But I stuffed my hands in my pockets and just said, 'Hi!' as if I met celebrities every day.

We followed Tiger Lilly down the hall and into a fantastic room with big comfy chairs and a dangly chandelier.

'Well, Damian,' she said, as she poured us some tea. 'I've got a little brother and he's always in trouble, too!'

'It may seem like trouble to some,' I said, darkly. 'But the fact is I work undercover. I'm a Private Eye.'

I could see she was dead impressed.

'I track down crooks . . . bank robbers . . . forgers . . . that kind of thing.'

Tiger Lilly turned and looked at Mum.

'You didn't tell me you've got your own detective agency, Mrs Drooth!' she said. Then she winked – or maybe she had something in her eye. 'He'll be useful on the day of the wedding. Don't want any of my presents getting stolen, eh?'

Mum looked horrified. 'Oh Damian won't be here on your wedding day,' she said. 'I wouldn't want him here with all your guests around. He'll just get in the way.'

Cheek! After all the times I've helped out! Only a few breakages. Only a few mistakes. That's understandable, isn't it?

Luckily, Tiger Lilly *insisted* I went.
'You organise the food, Mrs Drooth,
and Damian can keep a lookout for
suspicious characters.'

Mum couldn't say anything, could
she? I had been employed as a private
detective at the Wedding-of-the-Year.

Chapter 3

There were three weeks to go before the wedding and I had to be on top form. I needed to sharpen up my sleuthing skills. In my Supersleuth Notebook, I had a theory of detection to help me in my work:
ANYONE WITH EYES SET CLOSE TOGETHER IS NOT TO BE TRUSTED.

(This was very useful in my first case – known for miles around as the case of the Disappearing Daughter.)

But one theory wasn't enough. After all, I could be up against hardened criminals at the wedding. I decided to spend the time studying detective stories. There were some great ones in my comics. Mum didn't understand, of course.

'Why not read a proper book?' she said. But I stuck to it regardless.

After ten days of serious study, I came up with:
ANYONE WITH A BEARD (PARTICULARLY A BUSHY ONE) IS PROBABLY UP TO NO GOOD.

Working out a theory is one thing. Proving it is another. This is how I did it. *(For those who want to pick up hints about detective work, I've copied out my notebook in my best handwriting.)*

MONDAY

Our teacher, Mr Grimethorpe, is off sick. They say it's stress. But how can that be? Teachers have it dead easy! If you ask me, he spends too much time shouting and thumping his desk.

Our new teacher is
Mr Symes, <u>WHO HAS A</u>
<u>BEARD</u>.

<u>TUESDAY</u>
Mr Symes is dead keen on
money.
He counts dinner money
twice.
He needs watching.

WEDNESDAY

9.15   MS counts trip money 3 times!!!!!!

9.30   MS puts money in his briefcase.

THIS PROVES HE IS A THIEF.

18

9.35 Work out cunning plan in back of maths book.

9.45 Put plan into action. Stuff briefcase under my jumper. Creep out of classroom when MS isn't looking. Go to find Mrs Frank our school secretary.

10.00 School office locked. No sign of Mrs Frank. Probably making tea and chocolate biscuits for the Head.

10.10 Hide briefcase in cloakroom. Will pick it up later.

10.15 Go back to class.

MS has a temper as bad as Mr Grimethorpe. He makes me stay in at break and write lines. FOR NO REASON. He is a real criminal for sure.

11.00 Police arrive. How do they know about the money? MS looks dead worried. No wonder!

THURSDAY

9.00 No sign of Mr Symes. I expect he's in prison.

I will not mention my part in his downfall to the police.

So my Theory of the Beard was proved. Now I could track down the craftiest criminal who dared to go to Tiger Lilly's wedding.

Chapter 4

On the morning of the wedding, Mum
was in a real flap. Me? I'd got my gear
together, my notepad and my pen –
and I was ready to take on the big
names of the underworld, if necessary.

'Damian!' Mum shouted. 'Don't
stand there in a daze. Help me get
these puddings into the van.'

I ask you! Does James Bond carry
puddings for his mum? No! But that
day, she was in a bit of a mood. So
I did it. I picked up a big chocolate
mousse and carried it as carefully as I
could. Was it my fault if the path was
uneven? Was it my fault if I slipped?

Mum didn't speak to me all the way
to Tiger Lilly's place. She just gripped
the wheel and frowned at the road
ahead. She was in a real mood.

When we reached the house,
there was a security man on the
gate. He was huge and wore a badge
with DEAN on it. I must say, I
was surprised that Tiger Lilly had
employed him when she knew I was
coming.

Mum stopped and wound down the
window.

'Catering,' she said.

'I need to see your passes,' said
Dean.

Mum handed her card out of the
window. I leaned over and flashed the
detective badge I had made the night
before. We were waved straight in. No
problem.

The lawn in front of Tiger Lilly's
house was filled with an enormous
tent (called a *marquee*). And there
were loads of people milling around,
carrying chairs and arranging flowers.
Mum parked the van behind the
marquee and started unloading the

food. She was dashing backwards and
forwards like a wild thing, carrying
trays and dishes, and got really out of
breath. If you ask me, she's not at all
fit. She could do with a good work-out
at the gym.

I offered to help but she wasn't

keen. She said she'd rather do it herself.

'All right,' I said. 'I'll go and look round the grounds for crooks and that.'

Mum gave me one of her looks. 'You dare get into trouble!' she shouted over a pile of vol-au-vents. 'I've got enough to think about without worrying about you.'

'Stay cool!' I said. 'I'm in control.'

Mum's face turned scarlet. Probably her blood pressure. It's best to ignore it. So I put on my shades and walked away.

It wasn't long before I saw a man who was dead suspicious. He was wearing a black suit with a white shirt and was carrying a black leather case.

Spooky! And – guess what? His eyes were really close together. (Detection Theory number 1.) If that wasn't enough – he had a BIG BEARD, too! (Detection Theory number 2.) I had hit the jackpot! This man was a mega criminal.

I did a quick sketch and made some notes in my Supersleuth Notebook. Then I followed him into the house. It was obvious he was planning to steal the wedding presents.

Chapter 5

I walked behind him with my back pressed against the wall. Just like detectives on TV. But, before I got close, somebody shouted, 'Hey, kid!' and a security guard grabbed me by the collar.

'What do you think you're doing in here, eh?'

I checked his badge (which said CURT) and showed him mine.

'I'm with Mum's catering company,' I said.

Curt grunted.

'I'm Tiger Lilly's personal protection officer.'

Curt laughed! What was so funny?

'Out you go, sonny,' he said, as if I was a kid. 'Go and find your mum.'

Of course, I did no such thing. I owed it to Tiger Lilly to watch over her presents. I walked away, pretending to head for the marquee. When I was sure that Curt had gone, I hurried back towards the house and sneaked down the side.

As I peeped in through a window, I saw the presents spread out on a table. Each one had a label showing who had sent it. There were masses of silver plates and goblets – stuff like that. There were old paintings, too, that must have been worth a bomb. But in the middle of it all was a fantastic diamond necklace. A large label said, 'To Tiger Lilly on our wedding day from Gary with love and kisses.' YUK!

Tiger Lilly was marrying Gary Blaze. I didn't know why. He was a football player with skinny legs and no hair. He was useless at everything except scoring goals. Why did Tiger Lilly fall for someone like that, I ask you? She needed a guy with laser brainpower. Someone who could spot a thug a mile away.

As I looked through the window, the man with the beard walked into the room. He stood and stared at the diamond necklace. It was obvious that he was going to nick it when the not-very-bright security guard (CURT) wasn't looking.

I worked out a plan. I ran round
to the front door, hid behind the ivy
and waited. Ten minutes later the
man in black came out and I followed
him down the path. Half way, he
stopped, looked at his watch and
started running towards the marquee.
Suspicious or what? But I was onto
him.

By that time, the reception was in full swing. The crook went round the back of the tent, lifted a loose flap and sneaked in. He was cunning all right! But he wasn't going to get away.

I hurried to the main entrance of the tent. Inside, everybody was eating and talking. I could see Tiger Lilly looking fantastic in a long white dress with flowers in her hair and silver nail varnish. Gary Blaze looked stupid in a blue suit. (What did she see in him?)

I looked round trying to spot the thief. YES! There he was. Hiding amongst the band. Pretending to play a saxophone. Very clever, I don't think.

If he thought he would get away with the necklace – he was making a *big mistake*!

Chapter 6

I had to tell Tiger Lilly what was going on. I knew she'd be dead impressed when she heard I'd saved her diamond necklace. I started running towards her but, before I could get near, a hand landed on my shoulder and a security guard (KELVIN) pulled me up sharp.

I yelled. But nobody came to help. They were too busy stuffing themselves with Mum's food (chicken and all the trimmings).

'What do you think you're playing at?' said Kelvin as he dragged me outside.

I started to explain. 'I'm tracking down . . .'

But before I could finish, Curt came dashing out of the big house shouting, 'Come quick, Kelvin! Quick!'

Kelvin dropped me like a hot potato and ran. I followed, of course.

Something was up!

'The diamond necklace has been nicked,' said Curt.

'I know that,' I said – just to be helpful.

The guards turned and looked at me.

'How do you know?' said Kelvin.

'I'm a Private Eye,' I said, holding out my badge.

They raised their eyebrows and smirked. But I ignored them.

'I was watching the presents when I saw someone take the necklace.'

(It was *nearly* true. I *almost* saw him. It couldn't have been anyone else, could it?)

I flicked open my Supersleuth Notebook.

'The thief was a tall, thin male with a beard, wearing a black suit, a white shirt and carrying a black case.'

They looked at me as if I'd crawled out from under a stone.

'Stupid boy!' said Curt. 'That's Dave. He plays in the band!'

I smiled, knowingly. 'Just a cover for his criminal activities,' I said. 'I reckon the necklace is in the case.'

They snorted and pushed me to one side.

'Ring the police, Curt,' said Kelvin. 'Don't tell any of the guests or the wedding will be ruined.'

Curt got out his mobile and dialled 999.

'As for you!' said Kelvin, turning to
me. 'I thought we'd sent you back to
your mother.'

He didn't let me explain. He slung
me over his shoulders like a sack of
carrots. Cheek!

I thought he'd take me to the
refreshment tent. But he didn't. He
took me to the van.

'Right!' he said, swinging open the
back door. 'You can stay there until
your mum's finished with the food.
Then *she* can look after you.' He flung
me inside and slammed the door shut.

44

I didn't have the energy to try to escape. Suddenly I felt weak. My blood sugar was dropping. My brain was slowing down. I knew it was the stress of chasing criminals – and lack of food. Luckily, I had spotted a chocolate gateau in the back of the van. It's one of my favourites. So I had a slice, in the interest of successful crime detection.

(REMEMBER THIS TIP: Chocolate gateau is excellent for energy.)

I felt so much better after one slice that I had another. The more I ate, the more my brainpower increased. It was amazing! Of course, I hid the plate so Mum wouldn't notice the missing gateau. I didn't want her getting upset.

Now I was ready for action.
Escaping would be no problem. The
lock on the van door was broken, see.
When Mum locked it up at night, she
had to put a chain round the handles.
She said it was cheaper than having a
new lock fitted. But the guard didn't
know that, did he? He thought he'd
locked me in. Tee hee!

Slowly, I opened the door and
peeped out. I was a few metres from
the entrance of the marquee. I could

see Tiger Lilly (still looking gorgeous) and the band on the far side. But there were security guards everywhere. It was almost impossible to get in without being seen. So how could I reach the thief and save the diamond necklace?

Chapter 7

Being a trained detective, I soon had the problem sorted.

Between the van and the entrance was a large trolley with the wedding cake on top. Perfect! All I had to do was distract the waiter who was standing nearby. (He was wrinkled and stooping – at least forty.) Then I would hide under the trolley.

'Excuse me!' I said, climbing out of the van. 'Somebody's looking for you. I can hear them shouting over there.'

The waiter looked puzzled but went off round the back of the van. That was my chance. I dashed across, lifted the cloth and slipped onto the bottom layer of the trolley.

The waiter was back in no time.

'Huh! Young 'uns,' I heard him mutter. 'Up to their tricks!'

Then he pushed the trolley into the marquee, across the wooden floor and stopped in front of the bride's table. Everybody cheered and clapped as Tiger Lilly and the bald footballer walked towards it to cut the cake.

That's when I leapt out.

'HOLD EVERYTHING!' I shouted. (I had heard a detective say this in a film. I thought it sounded good.)

'STAND CLEAR!' I added, just for good measure. 'THERE IS A CROOK IN HERE AND HE'S STOLEN A DIAMOND NECKLACE!'

I must admit, I was surprised Tiger Lilly didn't rush to my side. Hadn't she understood what I'd said?

Instead, security guards were running towards me from every corner of the tent like crazy gorillas.

I jumped back onto the trolley and, pushing off with one foot, I skimmed over the floor towards the band.

'IT'S HIM!' I shouted. 'THE ONE WITH THE SAXOPHONE! HE STOLE THE NECKLACE AND IT'S IN HIS BLACK CASE!'

At this point, the trolley ran out of control and smashed into the band. I whizzed through the air like Superman and landed on the stage while the cake shot across the floor leaving behind a lake of white icing and cream.

I stared up into the face of the crook. (His beard looked even worse close up.)

'GOTCHA!' I said.

But it was the man *behind* him who suddenly leapt off the stage and made a run for it. Unluckily for him, he skidded on the splodge of cream. His feet flew out from under him and he crashed onto his back like a beached whale.

Meanwhile, I clambered across the stage and reached in his case.

'I think he's forgotten something,' I called out and held up the necklace for all to see. Now everybody was on their feet. They stood in a great circle round the crook, pushing and shoving to get a better look.

All this excitement – and then the police arrived.

'What's going on?' said the Inspector. 'Have you caught the thief?'

'Thanks to this boy, we have,' said Tiger Lilly. 'This is Damian Drooth and he could teach the police a thing or two about solving crimes.'

As she spoke, she put her arm round my shoulder. I almost fainted with pride.

Chapter 8

I expect you're wondering how I managed to track down the jewel thief. After all, he didn't have a beard like my first suspect.

Well, I must admit there was a bit of a mistake. You see, I'm not brilliant at names of instruments and stuff. So when I shouted, 'It's the one with the saxophone!' I got it wrong. I should have said a trumpet.

For your information, this is a
trumpet . . .

this is a saxophone.

But it didn't matter. As it turned out, the man who stole the necklace *really was* playing the saxophone. Lucky mistake, eh?

As for Tiger Lilly, she was thrilled I'd foiled the crook. I asked her if she'd sign my CDs and she said, 'Oh Damian, I'll give you a copy of every CD I've ever made **and** sign it for you.' Then she kissed me on the cheek. That was a bit girlie for me but it was OK, really.

Gary Blaze went all smarmy and said, 'Thanks ever so much, Damian.' I think he's a wimp. He said he'd give me a football and he'd sign it for me. But I said, 'No thanks. I'm not keen on football.'

Everybody cheered me and they
made a great fuss. They asked me
what I would like to eat and made me
sit at one of the posh tables.

'Sorry, Damian,' said Kelvin when
he brought me two plates of food.
'We've run out of chocolate gateau.
Will strawberries do?'

It's the thought that counts.

When everything had calmed down and most of the police had gone, Inspector Crockitt came over to talk to me. I'd met him before. He tries to pick up tips on solving crimes.

'How did you catch him, Damian?' he asked.

I'm too modest to tell a police inspector how to do his job. But I like to help.

'I've got this theory about beards,' I said.

'Is that how you solved this case?' he asked.

I could see he was keen to know. 'Maybe,' I said, winking at him. 'But maybe I got lucky.'

They don't call me Supersleuth for nothing.

NO.1 BOY DETECTIVE

Seek out more mysteries with the No.1 Boy Detective!

The Disappearing Daughter

Barbara Mitchelhill
Illustrated by
Tony Ross

The Popstar's Wedding

Barbara Mitchelhill
Illustrated by
Tony Ross

How To Be a Detective

Barbara Mitchelhill
Illustrated by
Tony Ross

Spycatcher

Barbara Mitchelhill
Illustrated by
Tony Ross

Serious Graffiti

Barbara Mitchelhill
Illustrated by
Tony Ross

Dog Snatchers

Barbara Mitchelhill
Illustrated by
Tony Ross

Under Cover

Barbara Mitchelhill
Illustrated by
Tony Ross

Gruesome Ghosts

Barbara Mitchelhill
Illustrated by
Tony Ross

Football Forgery

Barbara Mitchelhill
Illustrated by
Tony Ross

The Mega Quiz

Barbara Mitchelhill
Illustrated by
Tony Ross

Collect them all!